This Ladybird Book
belongs to

....

LADYBIRD BOOKS

UK | USA | Canada | Ireland | Australia | India | New Zealand | South Africa
Ladybird Books is part of the Penguin Random House group of companies
whose addresses can be found at global.penguinrandomhouse.com.
www.penguin.co.uk   www.puffin.co.uk   www.ladybird.co.uk

Penguin
Random House
UK

First published 2021
001
Adapted from Clement Clarke Moore's original poem,
A Visit from St Nicholas, by Libby Walden
Illustrated by Zeynep Özatalay
Text and illustrations copyright © Ladybird Books Ltd, 2021
Printed in China

The authorized representative in the EEA is Penguin Random House Ireland,
Morrison Chambers, 32 Nassau Street, Dublin D02 YH68

ISBN: 978–0–241–47907–0

All correspondence to:
Ladybird Books, Penguin Random House Children's
One Embassy Gardens, 8 Viaduct Gardens, London SW11 7BW

MIX
Paper from
responsible sources
FSC
www.fsc.org
FSC® C018179

THE NIGHT BEFORE CHRISTMAS

This is an adaptation of the original
festive poem, *A Visit from St Nicholas*,
by Clement Clarke Moore.

Adapted by
Libby Walden

Illustrated by
Zeynep Özatalay

'Twas the night before Christmas,
when all through the house
not a creature was stirring,
not even a mouse.

The stockings were hung by the chimney with care,
in the hope that Saint Nicholas soon would be there.

The children were nestled all snug in their beds,
as visions of sugarplums danced in their heads.

Then from outside the house
there came such a clatter,
and I leapt from my bed
to see what was the matter . . .

I ran to the window; I flew like a flash –
tore open the curtains and threw up the sash.

And what to my wondering
eyes should appear,
but a miniature sleigh
and eight tiny reindeer!

The little old driver was lively and quick –
I knew that it must be the magic Saint Nick.

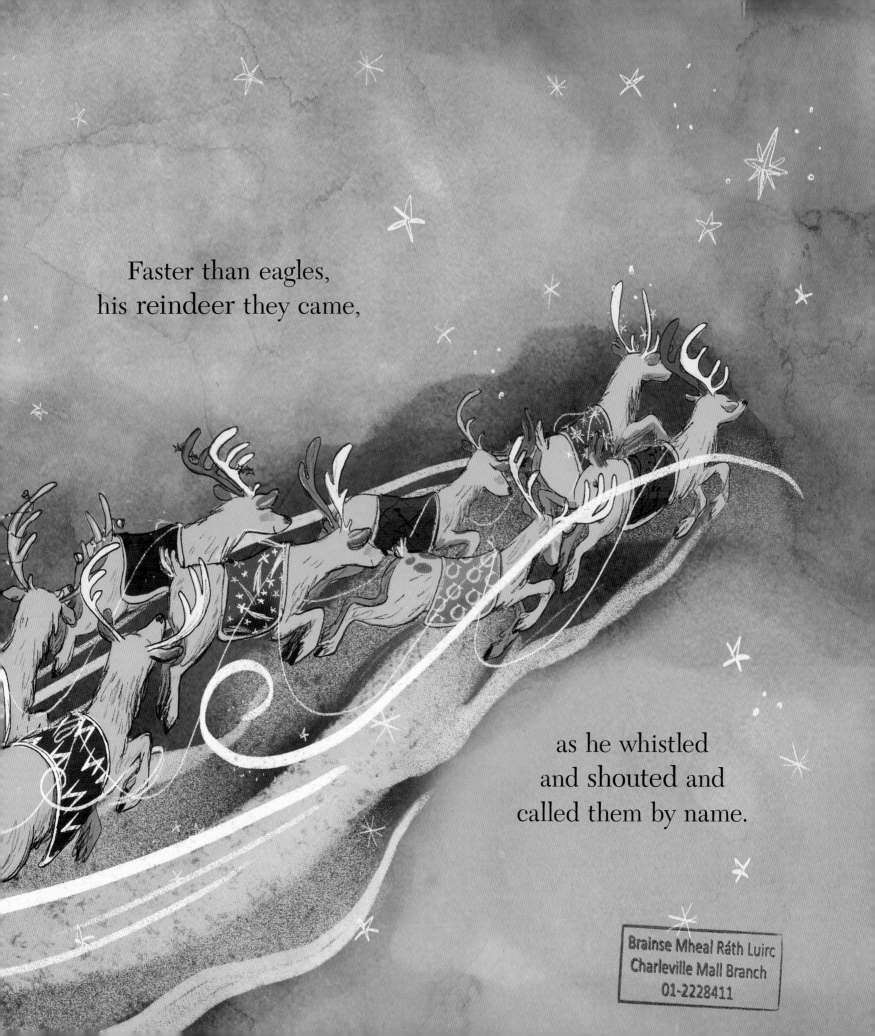

Faster than eagles,
his reindeer they came,

as he whistled
and shouted and
called them by name.

"Now, Dasher!

Now, Dancer!

Now, Prancer and Vixen!

On, Comet!

On, Cupid!

On, Donner and Blitzen!

To the top of the chimney and the top of the wall!
Now dash away! Dash away! Dash away all!"

Through the night sky the reindeer all flew,
with the sleigh full of toys, and Saint Nicholas too.

I then heard a twinkling, high up on our roof –
and the prancing and pawing of each little hoof.

As I walked from the window,
I heard a loud sound –
Down the chimney Saint Nicholas
came with a bound.

He was dressed all in red,
from his head to his foot,
and his clothes were all tarnished
with ashes and soot.

His eyes –
how they twinkled!

His dimples – how merry!

His cheeks were like roses,
his nose like a cherry!

His sweet little mouth was drawn up like a bow,
and the beard on his chin was as white as the snow.

He had a broad face and a little round belly,
that shook, when he laughed, like a bowl full of jelly.

He was joyful and festive, a jolly old elf,
and I laughed when I saw him, in spite of myself!

He said not a word,
but went straight to his work,
and filled all the stockings . . .

. . . then turned with a jerk!

He lifted a finger
to the side of his nose,

and giving a tap, up the chimney he rose.

He sprang to his sleigh
and gave a loud whistle,

and away they all flew
like the down of a thistle.

But I heard him shout out, as he drove out of sight . . .

"Merry Christmas to all,
and to all a good night!"